How to Make a Monster Smile

By Tomi Schwandt

For the ones who make me smile—Jamie, Ella, and Jack.

T.S.

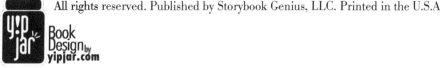

Hello, I feel happy!
How about you?
How do you feel?

Ah-ha! I see a monster has a case of the Grumpies.

My friend Monster feels quite dumpy. Let's work together to make him smile!

Start at your head and then move down low. Shake out those Grumpies! There you go!

A big hug

is sure to make him grin.

NOW, YOU squeeze someone tight

like your mom, dad or a friend!

Things are going mighty fine.

Let's do this ONE in double time.
Flap your arms and touch your toes.

Spin in a circle, then honk your nose!

I think we could use a good laugh.

Knock! Knock! Who's there?

A purple-spotted giraffe,

wearing his grandma's underwear!

Wait, just a minute! Surprise! He's right here!

Monster, you are catching on.
That frown of yours is almost gone!

Now try to **smile**
from ear to ear.
Once you do it,
let out a cheer!

We have covered a lot of ground and I must ask, do you ever feel the need to jump up and down or curl up in a ball and roll around?

How about we try this?

Snort like a pig.

Buzz like a bee.

Pucker up

like a fish in the sea.

Our work here together is almost complete.
I have just a few more tricks and those
Grumpies will see defeat.

Clap your hands.

Stomp your feet.

Blow a kiss.

Aren't you sweet!

Stand up tall. Count to three.

And with a big smile shout,

"I'm happy!"

You have made
a monster smile!

Now how about you?

Are you smiling, too!?

CPSIA information can be obtained
at www.ICGtesting.com
Printed in the USA
JSHW041959241120
9807JS00004B/54